Adventure in
the Caribbean

Adventure in the Caribbean

Stacy Towle Morgan

Illustrated by Pamela Querin

BETHANY HOUSE PUBLISHERS
MINNEAPOLIS, MINNESOTA 55438

Adventure in the Caribbean
Copyright © 1996
Stacy Towle Morgan

Cover and story illustrations by Pamela Querin

Published by Bethany House Publishers
A Ministry of Bethany Fellowship, Inc.
11300 Hampshire Avenue South
Minneapolis, Minnesota 55438

Printed in the United States of America.

Library of Congress Cataloging-in-Publication Data

Morgan, Stacy Towle.
    Adventure in the Caribbean ; Stacy Towle Morgan.
        p.   cm. — (The Ruby Slippers School ; 1)
    Summary: Eight-year-old Hope and her family travel to Antigua where they meet a descendant of slaves, learn that God is worshipped differently in different places, and find a long-hidden treasure.

    [1. Christian life—Fiction. 2. Antigua—Fiction.
3. Buried treasure—Fiction. 4. Slavery—West Indies—Fiction.] I. Title. II. Series: Morgan, Stacy Towle.
Ruby Slippers School ; 1.
PZ7.M82642Ad   1996
[Fic]—dc20   95–43934
ISBN 1–55661–600–7   CIP
                                                          AC

To my husband Michael—

my traveling companion

in life and love.

STACY TOWLE MORGAN has been writing ever since she was eight, when she set up a typewriter in the closet of the room she shared with her sister. A graduate of Cedarville College and Western Kentucky University, Stacy has written many feature articles and several books for children. Stacy and her husband, Michael, make their home in Indiana, where she currently spends her days home-schooling their four school-aged children in their own Ruby Slippers School.

Ruby Slippers School

Adventure in the Caribbean

The Belgium Book Mystery

Prologue

Hello! My name is Hope Vivian Brown. Vivian is the part I like, but Mom and Dad won't let me change my name to Vivian. I am eight and one-quarter years old. I live with my sister, Annie, who is six and three-quarter years old, and my mom and dad (who don't talk about how old they are!). We live in Chicago—the "Windy City." Dad has a job where he travels a lot. Usually, he gets to take us with him, so I joke that we like to go where the wind takes us.

Oh yes, I forgot to mention—I'm home-schooled, so my schoolwork travels with me in my old purple backpack. On our trips, lots of people ask me why I'm not in school. I just smile, turn around, and let them read the back of my pack: "Ruby Slippers School," it says. "Because there's no place like home." That usually explains things.

The best part about traveling is that I always learn something new, something I probably wouldn't have learned from a book. My favorite place to go is usually the one I just came back from. We got back yesterday from a great trip. I can't wait to tell you about it!

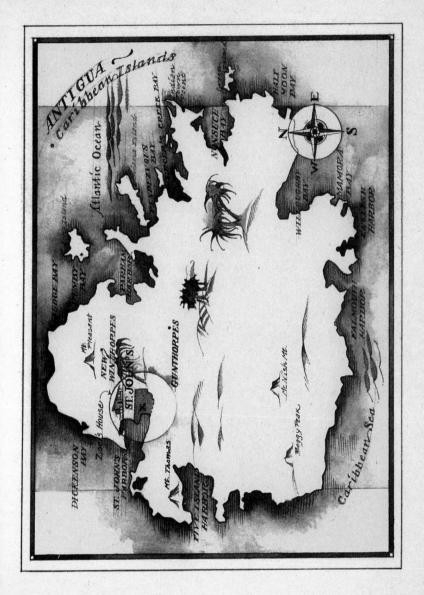

Chapter One

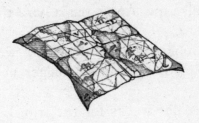

It was snowing the night before we left. I cleared a patch of frost from my bedroom window and imagined I was looking at a snow beach. The snow breezes swept into snow dunes. The air was filled with an icy spray that crashed against the houses. It was the best beach I could muster—at least until the next day.

You see, the next morning we were going to a real beach . . . very far away. It was Thanksgiving vacation and Dad and Mom were taking us to the Caribbean on something we call a "pleasurable business trip." That means that most of the time Dad works and we play.

I'll never forget the day Dad told us.

"Where's that?" Annie asked.

"Well, Antigua is a little island in the Caribbean," said Dad. "Right about here. Yes, there it is."

Annie and I squinted at the map. "Move your finger, Daddy," I said. "I can't see it."

Annie looked up. "It's awfully small. Can we all fit?" Unlike me, Annie has a hard time imagining anything.

"It just looks small on the map, sweetheart," Mom explained. "It's much bigger in real life. You'll see."

I planned for weeks for the trip. I practiced saying the words Caribbean (care-uh-BEE-un) and Antigua (An-TEE-guh) over and over again. I read lots of books about the West Indies and all about volcanoes and tropical storms. And I could almost guarantee I could find the island of Antigua on a map in less than thirty seconds.

"C'mon, girls. We need to get all the bags downstairs if we're going to make it on time," Dad said as he passed my bedroom door the next morning. "Hope, make sure you pack your journal. You'll have lots of things to write about while we're there."

I gathered all my things. At the last minute, I stuck Ellsworth, my bear, into my backpack. He was a gift from my Nana Brown when I was four years old (she has a teddy bear or two herself). I never take a trip without him. "There you go, Ellsworth," I said. "Last one in, first one out." In a

RUBY
SLIPPERS
SCHOOL

BECAUSE THERE'S NO
PLACE LIKE HOME.

whisper I added, "Don't be afraid of that X-ray machine at the airport. I promise I won't tell anyone your head's full of stuffing."

Annie poked her head in the door. "Are you talking to that bear again?" she said, as if *she* were the older sister. "You know bears don't talk or listen." Flopping down on the bed, she picked Ellsworth up out of my pack by one ear. She peered into it. "*Of course* his head is full of stuffing. What do you expect?"

"I expect you not to listen in on my conversations," I said, returning Ellsworth to his place of honor in the top of my backpack. "You wouldn't understand, anyway. You have no imagination."

"Well, *you* have no brains," she replied.

There was a long silence. Sometimes I wonder what planet she came from. We couldn't be more different. If we weren't related, we probably wouldn't even be friends. Nana would understand. I've caught her talking to her own bears.

"Let me try to explain, Annie," I said in hopes of making peace. "Have you ever looked at a picture and thought it said something to you? How about the last time we were at the ocean. Didn't the waves crashing against the shore say something to you?"

"Yes. They said, 'It's almost high tide. You'd

better move your towel, or it's going to get wet!' "

"Ugh! Never mind." I couldn't explain any-thing to Annie. "We'd better get downstairs with this luggage before Dad has a fit."

Chapter Two

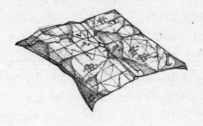

As the plane took off, I looked out the window at the buildings below. Tiny cars moved slowly on the frosted ground. I could even see tiny people shoveling snow in their tiny driveways. Pretty soon Chicago didn't look any bigger than Antigua on the map.

When I look out of an airplane window at the world below, I wonder how God sees me. I'm just a tiny speck, but He can watch me from far away. The Bible says He even knows how I *feel* about things—like when Annie grabs a snow sled away from me without asking. I may look small, but I know I'm pretty important!

During the plane trip, I remembered what I had learned about Antigua from the encyclopedia at home. I knew that the island had beautiful beaches with lots of white sand. I knew, too, that farmers there raised sugarcane to earn money.

But what I really wanted to know was what the food tasted like and what kinds of beds people slept in. I imagined hammocks hung about the rooms of their houses and piles of coconuts in the corner. And what about school? If it was hot all the time, how could they have summer vacation?

"Flight attendants, prepare for arrival," the pilot said. I leaned over and watched as the ground came closer. The palm trees grew bigger and the specks of cars and people went from being ants to life-size.

I leaned forward in my seat and whispered loudly to Annie across the aisle. "Annie, look at Antigua now," I said, pointing at the window. "Looks like we'll fit on this island just fine."

———

"Where you headed?" asked the taxi driver in his smooth voice. The taxi squealed out of the airport. One thing was sure: We were headed for the ride of our lives!

Dad braced himself. "Hold on to your hats, girls." I squeezed Ellsworth so tightly he could hardly breathe. The roads were bumpy and winding. And we rode around corners at race-car speeds.

"I guess there's no real speed limit around here," Mom yelled back to us over the noise of the honking horn. The driver dodged goats and pigs that wandered into the road. We almost hit one goat on its way somewhere.

"Look, Dad," I said, pointing to a particularly grungy goat, "I hope he's not going to the same hotel we are!"

When we finally reached the hotel, it didn't take long to settle in. "Take a few minutes to unpack, and then we'll go right down to the beach," Mom announced. Ellsworth was dying for a look at the ocean, so I hurried up just for him. "Only take your towel and your hat, Hope. I wouldn't want you to lose your bear on the beach."

Mom smiled. I think she understood about Ellsworth. "I'll tell you what. Why don't you put some sunscreen on Annie while I change? Make sure you cover her shoulders well. Antigua is close to the equator, so it's easy to get a terrible sunburn in very little time."

I placed Ellsworth gently on the bed pillow. His floppy head toppled forward. "Oh, Ellsworth, don't be upset. I'll be back soon, and I'll tell you all about it. I always do, don't I?"

Annie looked at me. She didn't say anything. "Here's the goop," she said, tossing me the lotion. I squeezed a glob of sunscreen on her shoulder and started to rub it in.

"You know, Hope, I guess it's OK if you talk to your bear. I know Nana does."

"It's all right," I said, drizzling a line of lotion down her back. "Bears don't talk to just anyone."

Annie turned her head and smiled, "Maybe when I get older, huh?"

"Yeah, I think you're too young to understand."

"Too young to understand what?" Dad said as he came out of the bathroom.

"Nothing, Dad. It's one of those sister things," I said. By the look on his face, I knew he didn't have any idea what we were talking about.

We picked up our towels and started for the door. "C'mon, Annie, let's go see what the beach has to say," I said, glancing back at Dad.

"It's definitely calling me!" he added.

Mom followed behind. "Me too!"

Chapter Three

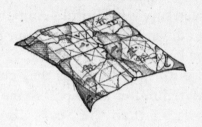

I don't think I'll ever forget my first close look at that ocean. It was sun-sparkle blue. When I leaned to look in the water, I could see fish swimming at the bottom. I stood in the white sand of Runaway Beach and smiled. God's world sure was beautiful!

"You three find a nice spot to settle," Dad said. "I'll go find some equipment for us to do some snorkeling. The bay at Runaway Beach is a good place for beginners to start."

"OK, Dad. We won't *run away!*"

"Very funny."

"Hurry back. We can't wait!" Annie said excitedly. We watched him walk across the beach toward a dive shop.

"Mom, it doesn't really feel like Thanksgiving

without turkey and stuffing and your famous marshmallow salad," I said.

"I know what you mean. But I was just thinking that without all that holiday busyness, I have more time to be thankful."

"The ocean sure is beautiful," Annie said, digging her toes down into the sand. "But those big waves can be kind of scary."

I looked out at the waves as they curled and splashed one right after another. "Some of those waves look taller than the Sears Tower back home!"

"Yes, they are pretty powerful," Mom agreed. "Make sure you always have a partner when you go into the water. The undertow can be very strong. I wouldn't want anything happening to either of you."

I nodded my head and looked at Annie with her strawberry blond hair and freckles. I was thankful for her. If we had been at home eating Thanksgiving turkey, I probably wouldn't have thought of that. Watching those huge waves made me want to take care of her. I never wanted to take it for granted that she was my sister.

Soon Dad came walking back to the beach. He looked like some sort of colorful octopus.

"Hey there! You ready to do a little snorkeling?"

"Well, aren't you a strange fish! What tide

26

washed you in?" teased Mom.

"Just help me out here, Gail. I've about lost feeling in my fingers carrying this stuff."

We grabbed our gear and started to sort out what went where.

Dad took over. "Now listen carefully. Let me give you a few instructions before we start. This tube here is called the snorkel. It attaches to your face mask like this. The snorkel lets you breathe while your face is underwater, so you want to make sure it sticks up out of the water."

Annie and I each placed a mask over our faces and one end of the tube into our mouths. We started doing sign language to each other and laughing.

"Divers do have their own sign language," Dad said, "but you'll be swimming near the surface. You can just remove your snorkel and talk above water when you want to say something."

"You're a good coach, Dad," I said. "Is there anything else we need to know? I can't wait to jump in!"

"Just make sure you breathe evenly and deeply. Hold your breath if you're going to swim below the surface. If you don't, the water will get into the tube, and you'll be in for trouble. Your mom and I will be right next to you in case there's a problem.

"One more thing," he added. "Before you

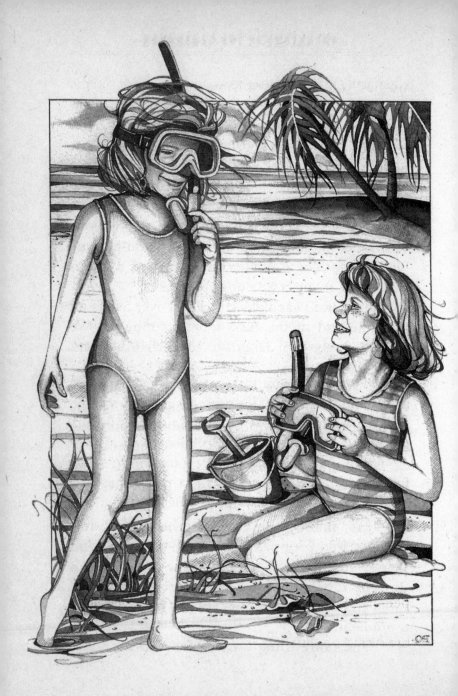

wear your mask under the water, you have to spit into it so it won't fog up."

"Yuk, that's gross," I said.

"It may be gross, but it works. Think of it this way—this is one time you can spit without getting in trouble!"

We started toward the calmer waters of the bay with our fins on. It took a lot of work just to walk. Dad yelled from behind. "Girls, pick up your feet nice and high."

"Just pretend you're stepping over the mess all over your bedroom floor," Mom added.

The closer I got to the water, the faster my heart beat. I loved to swim, but I wasn't sure I could do this. In swimming class, I was taught to hold my breath underwater. Now with my mask and snorkel, it was OK to breathe, but I wasn't sure I could make myself. I was afraid water would get into my mask or tube, and I'd drown.

I knelt down in the shallow water and put my face into the ocean. As soon as I tried to take a breath, I couldn't. It felt as if someone had put a towel on my face and wouldn't let go. I stood up in the water, spit out the mouthpiece, and gasped. "Daddy! Daddy!"

"It's OK, Hope, I'm right here. What happened?" I felt Dad's strong arms around me.

"I don't think I can do this. I'm not used to breathing underwater."

"I know, Hope, but it really is easy if you just relax. Let the snorkel work. Trust me."

"It's hard to trust. I want to, but it doesn't seem natural." I looked over and saw Annie's snorkel sticking up in the air. "How come Annie isn't having any trouble? She's younger than I am!"

"That's just the point. The older you get, the harder it is to trust."

Just then Annie popped her head up out of the water. "Oh, Hope, it's beautiful down there. C'mon. You have to see! You won't believe the colors, and the fish, and the plants!"

"Well, here goes nothing." I took a deep breath and placed the snorkel in my mouth. I plunged my head beneath the surface. Suddenly I was in another world—one I had only read about in books. I could hear my own breathing. My breath went in and out in steady rhythms.

I signed a thumbs-up to Annie. She pointed at a fish she wanted me to see. Only a few inches away was a spectacular yellow fish with purple stripes. It was amazing! Right behind him was a school of tiny black-and-yellow fish. Next to them I could see a piece of orange coral that was as bright as a colored marker.

As I turned around, I bumped into a big hairy leg. I nearly jumped out of my skin! Sputtering, I pulled my mask off. I stood nose-to-nose with

Dad. "Sorry, Dad. I guess I wasn't looking where I was going."

"Hey, that's OK. How do you like the view?"

"It's beeeee-autiful," I said happily. "I can't believe what I would have missed if I hadn't listened to you."

Chapter Four

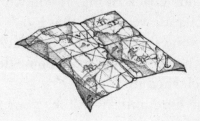

T hat was great," Annie said as we headed back to the hotel to shower. "I hope we can do that again."

"Yeah, I never imagined it would be so wonderful!" I said.

The hotel lobby was open all around except for the walls of pretty palm trees. As we passed the front desk, a lovely lady laid down her newspaper.

"Hello, Americans. Are you enjoying our beautiful beaches?" Her voice was mellow. It almost sounded as if she were singing when she spoke.

"How can you tell we're Americans?" Dad asked.

"You walk fast and you have American voices," she said with a smile.

"You mean we're loud," Mom added.

"That too," the woman replied very sweetly. "My name is Hyacinth. If there is anything I can do for you, please feel free to ask. We have boats to rent and horseback riding. If you would like a tour of the island, we can do that too."

"Thank you very much," Mom said in a much softer voice than usual. "We may come down later once we've cleaned up."

"I will be here until five. Take your time and enjoy."

As she picked up her newspaper, I noticed the headlines. In big, bold letters, it read: "BURIED TREASURE—Authorities on the Lookout."

"Did you see that, Dad?" I said. "There's buried treasure on this island. Just like in the books about pirates!"

"Hope, you are always looking for an adventure," Dad replied as he opened the door to our room. "See if you can find your sneakers buried in that pile of clothes by the bed. We'll go back down in a while and see if we can arrange a tour of the island for later."

After an hour, we stood again by the front desk. Hyacinth put down the sandwich she was eating. She seemed to float from her chair to the counter. "Hello again. What can I do for you?" she asked, leaning forward.

"We'd like to tour the sugar mills on Saturday afternoon," Dad said.

"Indeed. Sugar is our island treasure. We are very proud of our heritage," she said. "There are local tours on Saturday. They will be glad to show you around the mill and answer any questions you might have."

"Thank you," Dad said, then looked at me and winked.

"Speaking of treasure . . . my daughter Hope would like to see the newspaper you were reading. She noticed the story about buried treasure. Would you mind if we borrowed it for a few minutes?"

"Ah, an adventurer are you?" Hyacinth smiled. "I like that. Some people say there are treasures still buried on this island—although the coral reefs are treasure enough for me. Did you see the way the colors sparkle? They glisten like rubies and sapphires."

Hyacinth was right. The reefs *were* a treasure. I was glad to have gotten a peek at them. But I was still more interested in the buried treasure they talked about in the paper.

"Look, this article says searchers are looking for a treasure on the Falmouth plantation. Isn't that where Mom is taking us tomorrow for school?"

"So it is," Dad said.

"I have a friend, Mr. Desmond, whose ancestors worked on that very plantation," Hyacinth said. "Perhaps you will meet him if you go to market day early tomorrow morning. He'll tell you stories until sunset, but maybe he can help you find what you're looking for."

"Thank you, Hyacinth. We didn't mean to take up so much of your time," Dad apologized.

"Oh, we don't worry about time here. Everything moves more slowly." She waggled her finger and winked. "Americans are always in such a hurry."

Chapter Five

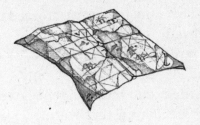

The next morning, we took a trip into the village for a look at downtown Antigua. It was market day. Dad promised to show us around before his afternoon meeting. Once we left the grounds of the big hotel, things didn't look like they had in all the pictures I'd seen—beautiful harbors, colorful gardens, and pretty shops. On either side of the road were broken-down houses painted happy, bright colors—pinks and greens and oranges.

"Do you think we could paint our house pink when we get home, Dad?" I asked.

"That's an interesting idea, Hope. We'll have to think about that." I didn't really expect we would.

We got out of the car on Long Street near the

square downtown to start our walking tour. The market had already been open for a few hours. Lots of people were crowding around the stalls. Hyacinth had warned us about the lizards (she called them geckos), so I wasn't surprised when one scurried over my foot as we crossed the street. Mom ran ahead.

"Boy, lizards sure can move fast," I said.

Dad smiled. "So can your mom!"

As we turned onto Independence Avenue, I realized it was becoming very warm. I wasn't used to such hot sun. To escape the heat, the people around us wore big straw hats or colorful scarves on their heads. Some even wore baskets of fruits or vegetables! I guess if I can carry school on my back, they can carry lunch on their heads.

At the market, I saw people sizing up the fruit and vegetables and choosing a fish to take home for dinner.

Then I saw something I didn't expect to see. An old man sat quietly reading the Bible at a table next to his fruit stand.

"Good day," he said, slowly standing and placing the Bible on his chair. "May I help you with anything?"

Dad started in. "As a matter of fact, you might. My family is here on a visit from the States. We're looking for someplace to worship Sunday morning. I noticed your Bible and wondered if you might suggest a church."

"Well, my man. It is a pleasure to meet a seeker like myself," he replied, reaching into a back pocket for his knife. He picked up a papaya and cut into the hard outer skin. "Try my papaya, and I will tell you a story."

He handed Dad a piece of fruit. "There was once a boy who loved bananas. Night and day this boy would eat nothing but the sweet, ripe fruit of the banana plant. Because he lived in a place where there were lots of bananas, he was happy. He did not understand how anyone could like the pulp of the mango or the yellow flesh of the papaya. 'Surely, you are all silly,' he said. 'You must eat bananas. They will make you happy.'

"But instead, he became unhappy because others would not eat the bananas he enjoyed so much. In the end, this boy grew to be a man of no joy. He could not eat or enjoy watching others eat. It made him mad. He starved to death."

The old man eyed them closely. "So, how do you like the papaya? Is it not a good, new sweetness to your mouth?"

Dad looked as if he were still puzzling over the story. "It sure is," he answered. "Try it, Gail." He handed the fruit to Mom. We all tasted it and agreed it was good.

The man continued. "Now, about a church. If you are looking for an American church, you will find one not too far from here—"

Dad interrupted. "Is there a place where we can worship with Antiguans? Maybe your church?"

"Ah yes." The old man smiled. "You and your family are welcome to come. Our church meets in the room above the photo studio downtown at ten A.M. You just go down the main street and follow the sounds of the songs. I warn you, though, our church is a fruit of a different flavor! We sing from our hearts! We will see you Sunday?"

"We will be there."

"Now, can I interest you in any of my fresh fruits and vegetables? Surely you don't have such fine fruit at home."

"That's very kind of you. Maybe you could help my wife, Gail, pick out something to take back for lunch. I have to leave now, but thank you, Mr. . . ."

"Desmond. You may call me Grandpa Desmond."

I thought he might be Mr. Desmond. His stories gave him away.

"Grandpa Desmond! How nice to meet you. A woman at our hotel, Hyacinth, told us we might run into you. My name is Reid Brown. This is my wife, Gail, and our children, Hope and Annie. I'm sorry I have to run, but I have an appointment."

Dad kissed us goodbye and waved for a taxi.

"I'll see you tonight after my meetings. Have a good day, girls."

While Dad was climbing into the taxi, a group of children passed behind him. They waved hello to the man at the fruit stand.

"Hello, Grandpa!" yelled a little girl in an orange-and-brown-checked uniform.

"Zoe! You are on your way to school? Come give your grandpa a kiss goodbye."

The young girl waved her friends on and started across the street.

"This is my littlest granddaughter, Zoe—sweeter than frangipani flowers. Zoe, I would like you to meet some new friends from the States. This is Mrs. Brown . . . and . . . I'm sorry. I have forgotten the children's names."

"Of course," Mom said. "This is Hope. She's eight."

"And a quarter," I added.

"And this is Annie, who is six."

"It's nice to meet you," Zoe smiled shyly. She looked over at me. "I am eight, too."

Zoe was very pretty. She had the smoothest dark brown skin. Her hair was braided in pigtails high on her head. She had a gleaming smile and glistening black eyes.

"Zoe is on her way to the Orange School." Grandpa Desmond turned to Zoe. "You better hurry up, or you will be late for class," he said,

patting her on the shoulder. "Now, see if you can catch up with Micheline and Beatrice. They're probably afraid I've twisted your arm to sell fruit today."

Zoe kissed him on the cheek, then looked at me again. She lowered her eyes. "Goodbye," she said.

I didn't want her to go.

Zoe's grandpa turned to me and drew me close to his chair. "You would like to be a friend of my little Zoe, am I right?"

I nodded.

"I think we can arrange that, if your mother agrees."

"Well, Grandpa Desmond, I would love for Hope to get to know Zoe. But right now we need to head off to Falmouth to learn about the history of your sugar plantations. School doesn't end for us when we travel." Mom laid her hand on my backpack. She gave me one of those looks that means school's in session.

"Ah yes, the sugar plantations. My very great-grandmother worked those fields some two hundred and fifty years ago. She was one of the few who survived those hard years of slavery."

"Grandpa Desmond, could we take you out to dinner tonight? I hope you don't mind my asking. I know Hope and Annie would love to hear about your family once they've visited the plantation.

Maybe you could bring Zoe along?"

"Even better, I will invite you to our home. I have some leftover papaya soup and some fish to fry. I would enjoy it more if you joined me."

Grandpa Desmond gave us directions. We promised to meet him later for supper. I could hardly wait for school to be over that day!

Chapter Six

The road to Falmouth took us through the rain forests. The trees were heavy with mangoes, pineapples, and bananas. We passed Boggy Peak, Antigua's highest point, and continued toward Falmouth Bay. I rolled down my window so we could all smell the salt of the ocean.

"That wind you're feeling is the same wind that brought people here from Europe," Mom said.

"This book I have calls them 'easterly trade winds,' " I said. "The wind brought ships from all over right past these islands."

Annie chirped up from the backseat. "We flew from one windy city to another, I guess."

"Yeah," I said, "but instead of airplanes, the traders came in ships. And it wasn't always trading that happened . . . at least not when they ran into pirates. The pirates took what they wanted—and what they wanted was gold and silver."

Annie suddenly pointed to a windmill in the distance. "Look out there!"

"I'd say we're getting close," Mom said. "That must be the sugar plantation up ahead."

I put my book back in my pack and looked out the front window. "You can tell it's a windy day, all right. Look at that windmill turn!"

We parked our car near the bay and looked out over the ocean. It took my breath away. As the clouds covered the bright sun, a shadow moved across the sea like a magician's hand, changing the color from blue to green.

"This is a great place to lay out a blanket and sit. Annie, you get the basket. You get the paper and pencils, Hope. I want you both to do some sketching."

Sketching pictures has always been one of my favorite things. It gives me lots of time to think. I reached into my backpack, grabbed my notebook, and began to sketch the windmill.

Mom sat down beside us. "I wanted you to see this." She handed Annie and me something that looked like bamboo but felt heavier.

"I've peeled some of the outer skin away near the top. Just suck on that top part, and tell me what you think it is."

"Is it sugar?" Annie asked.

"Actually, it's sugar*cane*, sweetheart. Now, bite down."

"Wow, the sugar really bursts out, doesn't it?" I said after chewing it for a minute.

"Exactly. That's why they had windmills. The heavy sugarcane was carried by slave workers to the mill. There the cane was placed between two heavy stones, which squeezed out the cane juice. Think of your teeth as the stones, pushing down hard on the cane."

"Mom?"

"Yes, Hope."

"Can we spit this stuff out? I think it's lost most of its flavor."

"Oh, I'm sorry, girls. I forgot to tell you not to swallow the cane. It's only good for its juice."

"So they didn't use the cane once they squeezed out the juice?" Annie asked.

"That's right. They threw away the cane and boiled the juice to get rid of any extra water. That gave them crystallized sugar and molasses."

"Oh, I love molasses in ginger cookies!" I said.

"They probably didn't have a lot of time to bake cookies. In fact, my book says that during the 1700s, the islands produced eighty to ninety percent of the sugar for Western Europe."

Annie was impressed. "That's a lot of sugar!"

"And a lot of work," Mom added. "Unfortunately, most of that hard work was done by slaves."

"Mmm . . . so that's what the trade ships were for," I said.

"Partly. But I'm sure Grandpa Desmond can tell you more. We'd better be getting back if we want to catch him in time for supper!"

The sun beat down on us as we packed our things and walked back to the car. I tried to imagine what it must have been like to carry loads of sugarcane instead of my backpack. I don't think that's a load *I* could've carried.

Chapter Seven

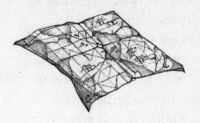

Grandpa Desmond greeted us at the door. "Come in and sit down, my friends. I was just about to put the fish in the pan."

We walked into the house. It looked like lots of houses I'd visited back home in Chicago. Sure it was blue-green on the outside and kind of small, but there was a couch and two chairs and a TV in the living room. On the wall above the couch hung an old sketch of a woman standing next to a house.

"Ah, Baba Ya has found you, I see."

"Is she the one you were talking about? The one who worked on a plantation?" I asked. Something about her eyes looked familiar. They looked like Zoe's.

"Yes. She is the one," he said, motioning for

me to sit down. "Her story, like her picture, has survived over these two hundred years. She came over as a young girl on a ship from a village in Africa. Her mother and father died during the trip across the Atlantic. Then she was alone."

"Alone on the ship?"

"Even though she was together in the ship with hundreds of people, she was alone in her heart. Baba Ya was sold to a plantation in Antigua, and here is where she made her life."

"Did she make friends here?"

"The story goes that Baba Ya met a white man—an indentured servant—named Aaron."

"What does *indentured* mean?"

"It means that as a young man he made a promise to work three to five years as a slave until he could buy his freedom. He came to Antigua to find his fortune. He hoped someday to own a plantation himself. While he was indentured, he belonged to his master—but he always hoped that he'd be free someday." The old man was quiet for a moment.

"When Aaron met Baba Ya, he was eighteen and she was eleven. He watched her bend under the weight as she worked carrying buckets of manure to the fields. He felt sorry for her—alone and struggling. At night he would sneak her extra food and water." Grandpa Desmond smiled.

"Baba Ya would thank him and say things like,

'There is nothing worse than to have hate as your master and be a slave in your soul.' Time and again Aaron was impressed by her wisdom and forgiveness.

"Aaron had been in Antigua two years. He had been treated poorly; he had scars on his back to show for it. But the black slaves were treated even worse. Aaron hated what the greedy plantation owners were doing to the slaves. In a place where sweet sugar was made, he only felt bitterness.

"Baba Ya did not like to see her friend angry. 'He who carries hate in his heart walks with stones in his shoes,' she told him.

"During the next three years of their friendship, Aaron grew to love a plantation owner's daughter named Victoria. As an indentured servant, he could not run away or marry without permission. He worked hard every day and longed for the moment when he would be free. Often he would whisper these words to Baba Ya: 'I promise I will make you free someday, for you have helped free my soul.'

"Three years later, he did. He married Victoria and took Baba Ya to his own plantation."

"Is that the end of the story?"

"A story never ends when there is someone left to tell it! Now, how about some fish?"

Just then the door opened, and Zoe walked into the room.

"Zoe, my little one! Come in and join us for supper."

"Mamma says I may," she said quietly.

Grandpa Desmond acted surprised. "You mean you would rather eat here with the girls than with your four brothers?"

She smiled and took a seat at the table.

Zoe leaned over and whispered in my ear. "After dinner, Mamma said you and Annie may come next door to my house and play."

At first I didn't want to have Annie come with me. I wanted Zoe all to myself. Then I thought of those huge waves and decided not to complain. I was glad to have a little sister.

Supper seemed to last forever. Grandpa Desmond talked more about the plantations and the history of the island, but I had a hard time listening. I just wanted supper to be over.

Finally, we cleared our places. Grandpa Desmond excused us from the table.

"You three run along and play. You haven't much time before dark, but the sun will rise again tomorrow."

We ran across the field toward her peach-colored house. Zoe opened the white iron gate and we walked in.

"Mamma! Mamma! Come meet my new friends," Zoe announced.

A tall, beautiful lady stood in front of us.

"Hello. My name is Mrs. Martin. I've heard all about you from my papa. I'm glad you could come and play with my little Zoe. She doesn't have any sisters, you know."

Just then four boys chased one another through the room at high speed. "You see what she's up against?" her mother laughed. "Zoe, maybe you'd like to show the girls your room."

We followed Zoe to her room in the back. I was surprised that she had some of the same toys as I did. We sat down on her bed, and I picked up a wooden box sitting on her nightstand.

"What's this?" I asked, opening the latch.

"That's a jewelry box that belonged to Baba Ya. It's very old. Mamma gave it to me for my birthday. It came with a special charm bracelet that I wear all the time."

"Oh, it's perfect," I said, touching the silver charm. "I have a jewelry box. So does Annie. Mine has a little knob on the bottom that you wind to make music."

I turned the roughly carved wooden box over and looked for a knob like mine. "I have a knob right here," I said, pushing my thumb against the hard wood. Suddenly the wood gave way, and the bottom panel fell out of the box! A slip of yellowed paper fluttered to the bed.

Chapter Eight

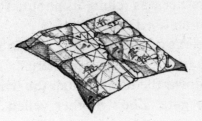

O h dear, I'm sorry, Zoe! I didn't mean to break it."

Zoe looked stunned. "You didn't break it, Hope. I think it was meant to be that way. I've always been careful not to push on the box because it's so old." She picked up the piece of paper.

Together we leaned over the paper to see what it said:

From Falmouth today
I must go away.
Buried east of the mills,
where the sugarcane spills,
is a gift from my heart
so we never shall part.
Love, Victoria

"And look, here's a map!" Annie cried. Sure enough, there was a map of the mill we had seen only that afternoon.

"Victoria," I said. "That must be the Victoria your grandfather was telling us about. You know, the one who married Aaron."

"Quick, let's go tell Grandpa. He could probably help us find what's buried there."

We ran down the hall through the living room and out the gate. Zoe's mother yelled after us. "You girls are as wild as the boys!"

The three of us burst into the house all out of breath. "Grandpa! Grandpa! You have to see this!" Zoe cried.

"Slow down, my little one. Nothing is *that* important. Come close and show me what you've got."

I handed him the piece of paper, and Zoe breathlessly gave him the wooden box. "Now this *is* important. Where did you find such a treasure?"

"Hope accidentally opened the bottom, and this paper fell out," Zoe said excitedly.

Grandpa Desmond turned over the box and looked underneath. "Hope, I believe you have outsmarted the pirates!"

He read the poem. " 'Where the sugarcane spills.' It must be that the treasure is buried underneath the ground where they placed the buckets to collect the cane juice. I know exactly where that is. I've stood there a million times thinking of the work Baba Ya must have had to do."

———

We planned to meet at the plantation site the next morning to dig for the treasure. Since it was Saturday, Dad would be able to come with us.

"Well, you girls certainly had a busy day. Looks like you're going to get your adventure after all, Hope," he said when we told him all about the box and the note later that night. "I can't say my day of meetings was anywhere near as exciting."

"I think they need a good night's rest if we're to get an early start tomorrow," Mom said in her practical way.

———

Annie turned the lights out, and I lay awake in the dark talking to Ellsworth.

"You wouldn't believe what happened . . ."

"Hope? Please go to sleep. You can talk to Ellsworth in the morning," Dad said.

"Good-night, Ellsworth," I whispered.

"I heard that," Annie chirped.

"I guess Ellsworth's ears aren't the only ones that work in this family!" I joked.

"Good-night, Annie."

"Good-night, Hope . . . *and* Ellsworth."

Chapter Nine

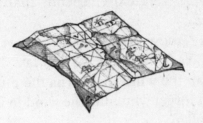

In the early morning, we all met at the top of the hill near the plantation windmill. The breeze was hot and dry. The ocean below looked cool and inviting. But we had work to do!

As the men and boys shoveled, Grandpa Desmond stood by with the map in his hand. He fanned himself with his big straw hat.

"Tell us the rest of the story, Grandpa Desmond," Annie asked.

"It is time you know the rest," he said. "Sit down and I will tell you.

"As you can imagine, Aaron soon grew tired of running a plantation. He treated the slaves with more kindness and respect than other masters, but he knew that being rich and owning slaves wasn't the most important thing. It was Aaron's dream to free his slaves and return to England.

"All the while Baba Ya worked tirelessly as the household servant. She took care of Victoria through yellow fever and typhus. It was said that no two people were closer friends than Baba Ya and Victoria.

" 'I don't know how I would survive without you, Baba Ya,' Victoria would say. 'You are stronger than the wind that turns the mill.'

" 'Don't forget who puts the wind in its place,' Baba Ya replied.

"In the third planting season, Aaron told Baba Ya of his plans to free all the workers and return to his homeland. 'Victoria and I would like you to come with us. We would like you to take care of us and the baby who is coming—as a free woman, of course.'

" 'The good Lord has saved my life to help my people,' she said. 'Thank you for all your love. It will be hard for me to say goodbye, but I feel I must stay.'

"So Aaron and Victoria left the island. Baba Ya became a household servant on a new plantation. That is where you see her in that picture."

"Did she ever get married?" Annie asked without thinking.

"Of course. She married a Desmond and lived to be nearly one hundred years old. A very long life for anyone . . . now or then."

Just then we heard the news we were waiting for.

Zoe's brothers started to shout. "We found it! Come here, everyone!"

We ran over to the spot where they had been digging. Leaning over the hole, Zoe yelled, "I see something."

"What you see is a big rock," said Grandpa Desmond with a sigh. "I'm afraid there's no chance of finding anything here. We've hit bottom."

We were all disappointed. Soon the tourists would be here. We had to get everything back in order. Grandpa Desmond told us that he had called the curator of the museum late last night to get special permission just to do what we had done. "I told him I used to own this property before I gave it to the island. I think I have every right to dig a little dirt if I please."

He sighed. "Well, we've dug some dirt all right. Now we need to get cleaned up. I am going to rest in the hammock behind the curator's office. I do my best thinking cradled in the arms of a hammock. Maybe I will learn the answer to our mystery in the breeze. The rest of you might as well go home. Just leave me a shovel."

Zoe and my family decided to stay for the tour. We would give Grandpa Desmond a ride when he was ready to go home. After the hole had been filled, we said goodbye to Zoe's mother and brothers and stood by the gate, waiting to take the tour.

The tour guide, Jasmine, took us through the plantation owner's house. We looked at the couch where the owner might have rested while servants fanned his face. We saw the room where owners visited with their guests from far away.

But the most interesting place was the servants' kitchen. Jasmine explained that the servants had their own garden. That way, they could grow their own vegetables in their spare time (if there was any). They could prepare them in the tiny kitchen they all shared.

On this day, there was a woman in the kitchen acting out how it might have been to cook back in those days. "Servants would bring in the water from outside," Jasmine explained. A woman dressed as a servant walked in with a heavy bucket of water. As she came in, she tripped on the stone step and water sloshed onto our feet.

"Excuse Baba Ya, she is tired from her day's work on the plantation." I was startled when I heard the name.

Zoe leaned over and whispered, "Grandpa insisted they use her name if he gave the museum the land." I smiled. Grandpa Desmond sure wanted to keep history alive.

Just then the curator stepped into the kitchen with a cup of coffee in his hand. He, too, tripped on the step and spilled some coffee onto the mud floor. "Watch your step," Jasmine cautioned. "As you can see, it's easy to trip."

As we all filed out, the curator stopped us to talk. "Excuse me. I am Christian, the museum curator. Mr. Desmond tells me you are good friends of his," he said, shaking hands with Dad.

"Actually, we just met yesterday. But we feel as if we've known Grandpa Desmond for a long time."

"Yes, he is a wonderful man. We are very excited about the possibility of finding his ancestors' treasure, but we are worried that you might damage something by digging. Maybe it would be better to take this to the authorities. Then they could look for the treasure."

I was afraid this would happen. We would be leaving after church tomorrow. I didn't want to leave Antigua before the mystery was solved. I was sure if we tried hard enough, we could find the treasure that day.

"Let me talk to Grandpa Desmond and see what he says," Dad offered.

"Thank you. I would appreciate your help."

"C'mon, Hope, it's not that bad," Mom said, putting her arm around me. "We've learned a lot while we've been here. I'm sure Zoe will write and tell you all about the search."

"But I didn't want to read about it, I wanted

to *do* it. I've already read lots of books about buried treasure. This was my chance to actually find one!"

"Well, sometimes things don't work out the way we plan."

Annie stepped out of the kitchen and added, "Besides, it's not as if the treasure is right under your feet or anything. It's probably going to take months to find it!"

Chapter Ten

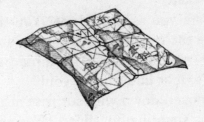

The sun was starting to set as we got ready to leave. Grandpa Desmond came around the corner to meet us with his shovel in hand. "Well, tomorrow is the Sabbath. There will be no digging on Sunday. Perhaps it's time to set out for home and prepare our hearts for worship."

"You're right, Grandpa," Dad said. "I'm sorry we won't be able to join the search team. I'd like to talk about that over a late supper. The curator has some ideas. . . ."

"Excuse me, Grandpa Desmond," I said. "Could I see that poem again? The one I found in the jewelry box?"

"What is it, Hope? Haven't given up hope yet?" Dad joked.

I stared hard at the words, " 'Where the su-

65

garcane spills . . . where the sugarcane spills . . . spills . . .' THAT'S IT! I know where the treasure is! It has to be! Of course, Victoria was thinking of Baba Ya, not herself. And the kitchen where Baba Ya worked."

"What are you saying, Hope? You think you know where the treasure is?" Mom said.

"You're standing right on it, Annie," I said excitedly. "It's right underneath you!"

Annie looked down with surprise at the stone step she was standing on. "Here? You think Victoria buried it here?"

"Yes. Don't you see? Almost everyone who has stepped through this back door has tripped. The water, the coffee—why not the juice of the sugarcane? Baba Ya could have spilled cane juice, right?"

"Well, it's worth a try," Dad said. "Annie, step down. Let's see if we can move this step."

Grandpa Desmond placed his shovel underneath and gave it a heave-ho. "It won't budge," he said. "We won't be able to move this without some real help."

"Please, Grandpa. Call the curator and have him get some help," Zoe pleaded. "It would mean so much to Hope to find it tonight."

"I have to admit, little one, I'm curious myself," Grandpa Desmond said. "I guess Christian will be getting another late-night call from me."

An hour later, the curator was there with five men to help move the stone from the earth. "I hope this isn't some wild goose chase you're on," he said to Grandpa Desmond as the stone popped from its place. It revealed sand that hadn't seen the light of day for hundreds of years.

"There you go," Christian said. "Here's a shovel. Good luck. I'm going to bed."

In the glow of the lanterns, Grandpa Desmond put a foot on the shovel and carefully scooped up the first shovelful of earth. It was like watching someone open a very important letter. Another scoop and another and still nothing . . . until the fourth time he dug the shovel into the dirt. The shovel made the sound of metal against metal.

"I believe I've hit something," Grandpa Desmond said in his slow, molasses-covered voice.

"Hurry up! Hurry up!" Annie yelled loudly in her American voice.

"Shh . . . there's no hurry," I said. I understood a little better now what Hyacinth meant about Americans.

Grandpa Desmond reached down slowly. He lifted a small metal box out of the dirt. His hands were shaking as he started to pry open the lid with his pocketknife.

"I see something," Zoe yelled. "It's gold and silver!"

Grandpa Desmond closed his eyes, nodded

his head, and smiled a slow smile. "I was right," Grandpa Desmond said. It must have been something the breeze told him.

"What were you right about, Grandpa?" Zoe asked.

"Victoria must have hidden her jewels before their trip so the pirates wouldn't get them." He turned to Zoe. "The jewelry box you have must have been a gift from Victoria."

"She probably hid the note in the box for Baba Ya to find, but she never did," I added.

"Look!" Annie exclaimed. "A bracelet just like yours, Zoe. And there's a note attached."

There in the tangle of jewelry was a bracelet exactly like the one on Zoe's wrist. "It must have belonged to Victoria," Zoe whispered. We all stared at it, imagining it slipped onto Victoria's slender, white wrist.

Chapter Eleven

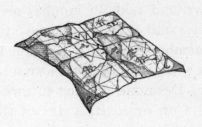

The next morning we walked into town for the Sunday service at Grandpa Desmond's church. The roads were empty and stores were closed. The closer we got to the photo studio, the louder the sounds of singing were. Up and down the street, songs floated through the air like a delicious smell.

Above the studio came the notes of "O for a Thousand Tongues." It was the same song I had heard hundreds of times at home. It sounded so different here, almost like a new song. There were drums and clapping and Caribbean rhythms. The song carried us up the stairs and into a small room. It wasn't much bigger than our living room at home.

"O for a thousand tongues to sing

My great Redeemer's praise.
The glories of my God and King,
The triumphs of His grace. . . ."

Grandpa Desmond stood at the door. He leaned down and said, "Churches are like the fruits in my stand. Lots of variety!" For a moment, I remembered the story Grandpa Desmond had told us when we met. That's what he meant!

Grandpa Desmond pointed to three rows of facing seats on opposite sides of the room. "There's some space over there."

We walked in and stood across the aisle from Zoe. I smiled at her and began clapping out the beat. This was nothing like our church at home. At home, things were so still and silent. There was so much noisy joy in this room. It was different, but I liked it.

We sat down after the song and read from the Bible we used at home. Suddenly it struck me. People all over the world were setting aside this same day to worship God in their own way—with their own voices and hearts.

I looked around the room at the colorful hats the women and girls were wearing. Many of them had handkerchiefs. A few had paper fans. Across the aisle in the center front seat was an old woman. It must have been a seat of honor, because in front of her was an electric fan that lightly blew her wispy white hair. I thought of Baba Ya.

She deserved a place of honor, too.

Annie nudged me in the ribs with her elbow. "A note for you," she said, passing me a piece of paper. I unfolded it and read: *Meet me under the chattering tree after church.*

I looked up at Zoe, and she smiled back and nodded her head.

As soon as the service was over, I looked for Zoe. I couldn't find her. "Grandpa Desmond, do you know what the chattering tree is?" I said.

"It is a place where old friends meet. You'll find it just beyond the stairs to the right. We call it a chattering tree because its pods hit together and make a chattering sound when the wind blows."

"Thank you!"

I walked down the stairs and found Zoe exactly where Grandpa Desmond said I would.

"I have something for you," she said. She took a handkerchief out of her pocket and handed it to me.

I opened one corner. It was the bracelet that had belonged to Victoria!

"I want you to have it," Zoe said quietly. "I never would have found the treasure if it hadn't been for you. You're a special friend."

"Oh, thank you, Zoe!" We hugged each other. "It will always remind me of you. I'll treasure it!"

I thought at that moment how treasures come in all different shapes and sizes.

"Mamma says we can use some of the money from the jewels to come see you in the States."

"I'd like that."

"Chicago sounds pretty big, though. A *lot* bigger than Antigua."

"It all depends on how you look at it," I said, sounding a little like my mother. "It's really not that big. It just looks that way on the map. You'll see!"

The End